ROOM
208

Rhesa Jack-Shallow

ROOM 208

Rhesa Jack-Shallow
rhesa.jack@gmail.com

ISBN 978-1-949826-46-3
Printed in the USA.

Published by: EAGLES GLOBAL BOOKS | Frisco, Texas
In conjunction with the 2022 Eagles Authors Course
Cover & interior designed by DestinedToPublish.com

DEDICATION

I dedicate this book to my husband and son. You both are my inspiration..

ACKNOWLEDGMENT

I would like to thank the Lord for the inspiration to compile this story. Truly, I can say I can do all things through Christ, who strengthens me.

I would also like to thank my husband, Gordon, who is my biggest cheerleader. I just have to say what I would like to do, and you're ready to give your support.

I would like to thank my son, Rhon, who is such an amazing child.

Thank you to my mom, Myrtle, who is the epitome of a stalwart who goes after her goals and achieves them. You inspire me more than you know, and I love you and appreciate you.

Thank you to my coaches Marilyn and Deborah, publisher and editor, in helping me bring this book into being.

CONTENTS

PREFACE

Believing in oneself doesn't come naturally to everyone. Besides fighting self-inflicted doubts, we are sometimes confronted with external doubt-spouters that can make us run for the hills and never take a chance on ourselves. However, as long as there is a passion for the gift that one is blessed with, there seems to come a time of emerging moments that define us—some for the better and some that make us want to retreat. These moments, I believe, come forth to test the integrity of our gifts and, once we've emerged unscathed, confirm the path that we should take,

Follow along with Rachel, a young woman with a gift for creating skincare products that have proven themselves effective in treating different ailments. She is highly recommended by her church sister Leah, and satisfied customers also endorse on the products. However, even with all the good reviews, Rachel doesn't feel confident that she can monetize her gift and change her financial situation.

Her doubts are also cemented by her boyfriend, Larry, who she holds in high regard.

In an unexpected turn of events, an unassuming stranger offers Rachel the opportunity of a lifetime, changing her perspective and dispelling her doubts forever.

CHAPTER 1

CELEBRATION TIME

ROOM
208

Cheers!

Hip hip hooray!

Congratulations!

The sentiments echoed around the room—Room 208.

Rachel surveyed the happy faces around the dining table and smiled back with genuine appreciation for the celebratory atmosphere. She'd hand-picked the feast in front of them from the menu the resort had sent her months ago, and she knew that this was just the first of the treats in store for them all over the next few days of their weekend getaway.

She sighed with satisfaction and pride as she reflected on the journey it had taken to be able to pay for this weekend in the beautiful, tranquil Caribbean, away from life's non-stop hustle and bustle. She'd chosen Room 208 because it was the place where she'd experienced the defining moment that got her to this time of celebration.

Room 208 and the resort was one of the most picturesque places one could ever expect to lay eyes on. There were three beaches on the resort with several shades of blue and the softest, powdery sand that you could set your feet on. The grounds of the resort was beautifully landscaped with grand palm trees and colorful flowers that attracted butterflies. From the reception lounge to the rooms screamed restful opulence. No expense was spared to make the guest feel welcomed and special. When they arrived, the friendliest staff had greeted them with warm hand towels to refresh themselves after the ten-minute boat ride across the turquoise-blue Caribbean Sea, and after being assigned their weekend butler, they were escorted by elevator to their wing of the resort.

The corridor leading to the room was beautifully accented with abstract paintings of everything sun, sand, and sea. Strategically placed plush chairs lined the corridor, accenting the pathway to the rooms. As the butler made a stop in front of the most gorgeous French doors made of teakwood, excitement and anticipation rushed through Rachel.

Rebecca and Rachel's mom gasped and their sound filled the corridor as both doors swung open and the beauty and opulence of the room hit them. Rachel knew it's because it was their first time experiencing such beauty. "Welcome to

Room 208," said the butler, jolting them from their awestruck moment.

"Thank you!" they chorused, as if they'd rehearsed for just that moment. Leah pushed passed them and went up to the window overlooking the sea. "Oh my goodness, look at this gorgeousness! I feel like I just walked into a dream." She exclaimed. Rachel smiled because it was exactly the impact she wanted to make on these deserving women who have always supported her.

To the left was a door leading to a kitchenette with modern appliances, complete with wine cooler stocked with fine wine. On the right, another door led to a powder room. Directly in front of them was an open space dining room and living room that drew the eyes out to the crisp waters of the Caribbean Sea. The floors, countertops, bathroom, tub, and other finishes were fine marble.

"Here are your room keys and the control pad console that controls the lights, drapes, and temperature of the room. You can use it to order your meals, and your vacation itinerary is also on it. Should you have any requests at all, just let me know. I'm just three minutes away." he said. "Is there anything else I can help you with?"

"No thanks," Rachel replied. "We just want to settle into our rooms and prepare for dinner."

"Great, welcome again and we hope you would enjoy your stay with us," He exited and left them to continue exploring their space.

There were three en suite rooms complete with seating areas, bedroom, walk-in closet, bathroom with a Jacuzzi and shower and a private toilet space. The ceilings were white with white crown molding that seemed to go on for days. From the looks of it, the linens were no less than a thousand thread count. Evidently, luxury was not denied, and Rachel would have it no other way. Each room had its own private balcony, complete with a lounge bed that faced the sea. After delegating rooms, Rachel asked the group to get some rest and gather again for dinner. Her mom and Rebecca would share a room, Leah and Annie the other and of course she would have her own room.

As Rachel unpacked her bags, her thoughts wandered to the women with her. Her mom, ever so deserving of this trip, had worked tirelessly to raise Rachel single-handedly after Rachel's father walked out. There was Annie, her childhood best friend, who she hoped would gain a different perspective of life after this trip. Annie rarely saw the positive in any situation. Rachel tried to be easy on her because she knew Annie's background caused her to be that way. There was also Leah, Rachel's church women's group leader. Leah always had an encouraging word for Rachel, unknown to Leah, often at times when Rachel needed to hear it most. Leah deserved this trip. Lastly, there was Rebecca, Rachel's sister, and always the life of the party. They barely got to see each other because Rebecca lived on the east side of the country, busy as an amazing stay-at-home mom and wife. Rachel was thrilled she could give her sister this trip to unwind and relax for a few days.

A soft knock jolted her from her thoughts. "Come in,"

"Oh my gosh!" exclaimed Rebecca as she plopped down on Rachel's bed. "This place is absolutely amazing, Rachel! Thanks for inviting me."

"I know, right? I couldn't imagine celebrating the success of my new business venture without you, sis. Even though you're miles away, you're always checking in on me," said Rachel, sitting next to her and throwing her arm around her shoulders.

Before she could say more, another knock sounded. This time it was her mom. Rachel and Rebecca scooted over and made room for her. Just like the old days, thought Rachel. Her mom had gone through so much after her husband walked out. She raised her daughters alone, without complaint. When they were young, Rachel had often had to babysit Rebecca when their mom did weekend jobs, but not once had she felt overwhelmed, because she had a sense of joy knowing that she too contributed to helping her mom raise them.

"Mom, are you okay?" Rebecca asked.

Rachel looked over just in time to see their mother wipe a tear from her eye.

"Yes," her mom whispered. "I feel truly blessed to have you both with me, and I want you guys to know that I am absolutely proud of the women you've become." She wasn't a woman of many words, so they both knew this was a special moment for her. They all hugged, cried, and burst out laughing, filled with the joy of being able to meet like this again.

"Come on, let's get ready for dinner. We have a packed weekend ahead," said Rachel joyfully. They didn't know about the big reveal she planned for during this trip. When they got to dinner that evening, the table was beautifully laid with fine china and cutlery. Even the floral arrangement set in the middle contained all of Rachel's favorite flowers. She realized that the resort manager had gone the extra mile to make sure that her favorite things were placed in the room. Everyone was content.

The following morning, Rachel got up at the crack of dawn to walk along the shoreline. She needed time to clear her head and get some much-needed exercise before the calories she'd consumed at dinner got the better of her. She'd been determined not to let any of it go to waste last night, and now she was determined not to let too much of it go to waist either. She chuckled to herself as she reflected that it was the first time she hadn't heard Annie complain about the culinary skill of a chef. All the women had nothing but high compliments for the chef and the professional service they'd received.

When she returned to the room, everyone else was up, showered, and making their way to the dining room for breakfast. She got a quick shower and put on her swimming suit and cover up in preparation for their boating trip.

Ping! went her phone. "Hey you, how's the trip going?" Flashed across her screen. It was David checking in to see how her trip was going so far. She smiled as she replied that she was having the most amazing time with her family and friends. She'd met David about twelve months ago and already felt like she'd known him for years. She owed this trip to him, and even the start of her new business venture, Glow Up. He was the most humble human she'd ever met, despite all his accolades. You'd never know he was a billionaire and real estate giant in New York, and the Caribbean of all places. But his success was never the focus of their conversations. He always gave sound practical advice, whether or not she liked it, and she developed an appreciation of his wisdom.

"I'll message you after our trip" Rachel typed back. She let him know she'd update him later after their boating trip and hurried to get breakfast with the other women. They all knew about David and often teased her, after Larry her ex-fiancé left, that maybe David would be the one. Rachel always told them she was in no hurry to find another man. She liked David, but she was determined to keep their friendship organic, just the way it started.

"Hey guys, don't forget our butler will be here at 10:00 a.m. to escort us to the catamaran for our sailing trip," she reminded them as she walked into the dining room. Leah and Annie had never sailed before, so she wanted to make sure they got to do so on this trip. Sailing was something she, Rebecca, and their mom got to enjoy because her uncle took them fishing once a year during the summer during their childhood.

"Will they provide life vests?" Leah asked nervously.

Rachel laughed. "Of course they will. And you've got nothing to worry about. It's going to be a great trip with experienced people in charge."

They spent the day sailing, learning to snorkel, dolphin watching, and sampling the fresh juicy fruits of the Caribbean and local foods provided by the captain of the catamaran. They couldn't have asked for a better way to relax and unwind from their regular day-to-day lives. The weather was perfect, and they enjoyed the feel of the salty water on their skin.

At the end of the trip, the women returned to their rooms pleasantly energized. Their rooms were refreshed and table settings were being prepared for the evening's fine dining. Rachel took a moment to savor the whole experience. If anyone had told her she'd be able to do this for her family and friends ten months ago, she'd have been in disbelief. But now here she stood, in this room, fully paid for at ten thousand dollars per night and didn't have to worry about blowing up her tab. Although she'd started working at the age of eighteen, she was never able to afford to go on vacation, and she'd relished the conversations of colleagues who went on vacation with their families.

It wasn't until she became a senior accountant that she got to take her first official plane ride, on a business trip to Florida. Back then she was nervous, yet excited, and challenged herself to create a list of places she wanted to visit in the future.

She smiled as she remembered how her life had changed so drastically in the past ten months. She'd launched her spa franchise, Glow Up, and her signature body-care line that was now sold in all the major malls across the USA. Her products had done far better than she'd expected too. Her journey hadn't been easy; she'd lost a lot: money, Larry, and a few friends. However, she'd gained a lot more: money, new friends, and the ability to transform her life.

After meeting David, Rachel had developed the courage to pursue her dreams. When they met, she was going through the motions of her job. She was excellent at what she did. Her boss loved her and she'd risen to the ranks of senior accountant in just two years after completing her studies. Her boss always gave her the complicated cases to handle, and she did a great job of handling them. However, she'd always loved giving spa treatments and taking care of her body with natural products. She made lotions, soaps, and scrubs then gifted them to her friends and taught them how to create their own personal retreats at home.

Her friends always raved about how much her products lifted their spirits and made them feel better. Rebecca used the products on her children to help overcome their eczema. Rachel loved researching natural ingredients and trying out new recipes to improve her products. However, that's as far as she went with sharing them. Larry had always told her it was a good hobby, but no one would really be into that sort of product on a large scale. He studied marketing, and she valued his opinion, so she listened to him.

Although Rachel was great at being an accountant, she'd always felt that there was a void, that there was more she could do and accomplish. She felt a longing and an emptiness that was only filled when she made her products. Eventually, she convinced herself that she'd keep her hobby as a hobby and be satisfied with her day job.

But then she met David and her life changed. She was standing right here in this moment because she had dared to walk away from that accounting job and pursue her hobby. Now here she was: small-time accountant turned business mogul.

This was truly her time for celebration, and she looked forward to surprising the women with the launch of her new Glow Up spa franchise at the resort, with the goal of growing it within the Caribbean. With luck, this would be their first of many trips to the Caribbean.

CHAPTER 2

ON THE JOB

"Listen, that's just the way things work, Rachel. My parents went through it; your parents went through it. You just do your best," Annie said as they took their lunch break at the café opposite Rachel's office. "You're young. It'll get better."

"OK, Grandma!" Rachel retorted. Annie never empathized with her when she talked about the struggles she faced at her firm. Rachel was sharing how stressful the last three months had been. Not only was her boss giving her the harder clients to service, but her colleagues weren't cooperating because they felt the boss favored her. This meant longer working hours. She was also feeling the impact physically, and her doctor had warned her that her high blood pressure was because of the stress.

"So you're saying that I shouldn't consider quitting?" Rachel asked as she chomped down on her chicken Caesar salad. Eating was also starting to feel like a luxury.

"You've always wanted to be a partner at the firm. You've been there for ten years now. How much longer can it take?" Annie replied.

Rachel shrugged. "You know how I feel about my skincare line. I don't feel as stressed doing that, and I believe my recipes are great. Rebecca told me the kids' pediatrician was impressed by how well their skin was doing."

Annie cut her off. "You want to throw away what you have for what you're not sure about? How do you know this is going to work? Take your head out of the clouds."

Rachel rolled her eyes. At the same time, Larry arrived and grabbed the empty chair. As usual, he was late. He gave her a quick kiss on the cheek and started looking at the menu. He ordered a chicken pasta salad and a Coca Cola.

"What are you two hens pecking about?" he teased.

"The usual. Rachel wants to leave the firm and dive into the deep unknown," Annie stated before Rachel had time to respond.

Larry looked at her, and she knew what he was thinking. They'd had this conversation several times before. He felt she should keep the job because it would bring more stability to their income when they got married next year. She looked at him and shrugged.

Thcy'd been together for five years, and he'd recently popped the big question. Of course, she said yes. They'd been together for a long time, and their families were wondering if they'd ever settle down. They lived in his apartment and were already making plans to buy a house so she could have more space to work on her skincare products.

Larry worked as a marketing executive at one of the top marketing companies in the city. Just like her, he was great at what he did. The only difference was he didn't experience half the stress she did at her firm. She valued his opinion, and she thought that's why she'd fallen in love with him. She enjoyed the smoothness and ease of conversation with him. They talked a lot about what they hoped their life would be like in the future. The only area they disagreed on was her going into business full time. Larry preferred, as he told her often, "the security" of working with a large organization and the prestige that went with the job. Rachel envisioned owning her own business, the flexibility to travel, be a present mom and wife, and the ability to be herself more. The day-to-day hustle of work was, frankly, boring and beginning to take a toll on her mentally.

She glanced up and smiled sweetly at him. "So how did your presentation go today? Was John impressed?" John was Larry's CEO.

"He definitely was. Not only did I get the job to create the marketing ad for the car company, but I also get to choose who works along with me on the project."

Rachel squealed. "Awesome! Sounds like a celebration later." She faked the clinking of glasses as her phone buzzed on the table next to her plate.

She grunted and mumbled as she stood and picked up her bag. She wondered if she really worked at an accounting firm or the emergency room.

"Leaving so eagerly?" Annie asked.

"I've got a meeting with Laura—something about needing information to present to a board..." She trailed off in thought. She had spoiled Laura by always being available. She made a mental note to develop better boundaries.

She kissed Larry and waved to Annie as she placed money for her lunch on the table and hurriedly made her way back to the office.

Laura was waiting for her in the conference room.

"What took you so long?" Laura asked as soon as she sat down. Laura was an unassuming woman. She seemed to never have everything under control, but she always found a way to please the customers. That's why the company performed so well and was renowned as one of the top accounting firms in the city.

"What do you need me to work on?" Rachel responded without answering her question. She knew Laura was intentionally trying to be annoying. Rachel was one of her top, if not the top, senior accountant in the firm, and Laura knew Rachel had her back when it came to supplying clients with timely deliverables.

"BCL Associates needs us to do a three-year projection of sales so they can make representations to their bank. They need it in two days." Laura replied without looking at her. Before she could respond, Laura continued, "By the way, get your swimming trunks out, I'm sending you to Anguilla next month to meet the director of the Oriental Group. They're looking to take over the LaLuna Resort there and need someone from the company to help them peruse the books to determine if it would be a profitable takeover."

As she was about to respond, Laura continued with her monologue, "Reynold and I were discussing the opening for partner coming up soon, so we'll be analyzing our seniors to see who'll be best able to fill the role." Reynold was Laura's husband and managing partner at the company.

Rachel gave a slight nod of acknowledgment. Was this the moment she'd been waiting for or was it just an attempt from Laura to pacify her so she wouldn't feel frustrated by all the workload that was coming her way? The upcoming trip piqued her interest. As much as she knew a lot of work would be involved, she welcomed the change of scenery—literally. She was overdue for a vacation, and she relished the thought of getting away from Larry a bit. They were on good terms, but she was growing weary of him complaining about the amount of space her skincare production was taking up. Didn't he realize how relaxed making her lotions and potions, as she like to call them, made her feel?

Out of curiosity, she asked, "How long would the trip to Anguilla be?"

"At least a week," Laura responded. "They're very serious about this takeover."

"Who else will be going with me?" Rachel asked.

"You alone. We don't want to spend any additional resources on this trip."

Rachel made an internal sigh as she grabbed the folder from BCL Associates. Her mental note to set some boundaries came back to her. Laura was asking her to do too much. She had to draw some lines.

"Let's begin," Laura's voice broke through her mental rant.

The following morning, Rachel jumped out of sleep to silence her alarm. She was near panic mode before she realized it was Saturday morning and it was okay to sleep in a little longer. She looked over to the other side of the bed and realized that Larry had already gotten up and, more than likely, was deep in his Saturday morning gym repertoire.

She groaned as a wave of headache enveloped her. She hadn't got home until 1:00 a.m. She'd stayed late, determined to finish the file for BCL Associates. She was very familiar with their files and accounts, so although it was tedious to compile, she didn't struggle with their information. She'd sent the completed document to Laura before leaving after midnight. Only the security guard was on duty as she left the office, because who stays late at work on a Friday night? No one, of course, except Rachel. No wonder Laura placed so much work on her shoulders. She over delivered.

An hour later, Rachel dragged herself from bed. Her headache had subsided a little. She took a warm shower, the natural herbs and oils from the soap bar she'd made lifting her spirits. She grabbed something to eat and scanned her recipe book, looking for a combination of items to present to the women's group's indoor fair in three weeks—a week before her trip to Anguilla. She decided on her signature vanilla soap, sugar body scrub, and cashmere body lotion . To ensure she had everything ready in time, she had to start making her items today.

By the time she'd poured her lotion and soap, Larry was coming through the door, thankfully with lunch in his hands. The entire apartment smelled of vanilla and cashmere, and her headache was gone. This processing was pure therapy.

"I don't even want to ask," Larry said as he gave her a quick peck on her cheek and set the lunch on the island, away from her production setup on the counter.

"Leah asked me to sell some of my body-care products at the women's group's fair in a few weeks. I told you this." She started to whip up the ingredients for her body scrub. "What do you think of this scent combination?"

He gingerly leaned in to smell the body scrub, but he couldn't deny it smelled great.

"I'll need your help with setup, and remember we're supposed to meet with the pastor afterward to discuss our plans and arrange a schedule to begin counseling," she continued.

Larry mumbled something in the affirmative as he scampered off to get freshened up.

Rachel had met Leah about a year ago when she came into the firm where Rachel worked, seeking an accountant. Rachel immediately liked her. Leah was unpretentious and serious about growing her catering business. She wanted to expand so she could employ more people. Leah wanted to hire teenage mothers who needed the income to look after their children. Rachel admired her nobility. Not only was Leah's business renowned for helping women, but it was incredibly successful, making at least six figures annually. What was even more admirable was that Leah was a Christian, and she too had been a teenage mother who'd turned her life around.

From the moment they met, they'd hit it off. Rachel was happy when Laura assigned her the task of helping Leah organize her books. Their friendship grew from Rachel accepting Leah's invitation to a birthday party she was catering for, then to a luncheon at Leah's house, a women's retreat in the mountains and of course, to church. Rachel felt like a kin to Leah. When Leah found out about Rachel's passion for making skincare products, she encouraged her. One time, Leah even spent five hundred dollars purchasing the products Rachel had made.

Rachel smiled as she recalled how she and Leah were once sitting at the welcome table at church when another lady commented on how fragrant Leah smelled. Leah didn't miss a beat and raved about Rachel's products. Through that one conversation, Rachel got orders from ten other women for lotions, scrubs, and soaps. It was the biggest demand she'd experienced, but she was more than happy to meet it. As a matter of fact, Leah was the inspiration for her business's name. She'd always ask people, "Do you like my glow up?" She insisted Rachel's body scrubs gave her a glow.

From then on, Rachel's popularity grew at church, and whenever there was a display, fair, or women's group activity, she was booked. Rachel enjoyed all of it because it gave her the opportunity to forget the monotony of her day job.

Her phone rang, jolting her from her daydream. It was Leah, checking in and trying to find out what concoction she was developing for the fair. They chatted for fifteen minutes before she tore herself away to ensure her tasks for the day got finished.

Fortunately, by the time Larry came back, she was finished and able to sit on the terrace of their apartment to have lunch with him.

The baked wings with tossed Greek salad were all she needed to fill her hunger. She really wanted to discuss investing in more equipment, but that conversation was always filled with tension. However, he seemed to be in a jovial mood, so she decided to go for it. She swallowed her mouthful and paused briefly before saying, "Honey, I've been getting more orders for my products. But I'm going to need more equipment to fill the demand."

His expression clouded as she continued. "Don't worry; we won't have to use savings. Rebecca and her husband want to help me get the equipment."

Larry relaxed a little at that, but, his frown remained. "I see there's no stopping you from going after this. But, Rachel, I'm really concerned about the demands it's putting on you." He said softly, "We barely get time for each other."

She knew that was one of his concerns, which was why she'd made sure everything was done before he came back to eat. "I know, but I can't ignore the benefits my customers have received from my products.

"You know what? You do what you want to do. I'm not going to have any more input in any of this. You're on your own, so figure it out," Larry responded angrily, almost breaking the glass he placed on the table.

Rachel loved Larry, but deep down she knew that this venture could be a deal breaker for their relationship. That's why she was in no rush to plan a wedding.

"By the way, why didn't you tell me that partner is up for grabs?" Larry asked. Rachel knew Annie must have told him. She'd briefly mentioned it to her friend.

"I just feel like Laura is dangling it in front of me to make up for all the work she's been giving me lately," Rachel responded nonchalantly. "She's even sending me to Anguilla for a week ... alone."

Larry raised a brow.

Rachel sighed. "Larry, I don't envision doing this forever. Being a partner doesn't mean the work will get easier. It'll be even longer hours."

"That may be so, but we wouldn't have to worry about how the bills will get paid. Plus, the commissions and bonus packages are unheard of."

Larry had a deep fear of failure. When he was growing up, his dad had a mechanic shop, and from his recount of his childhood, it was a struggle for his parents to take care of him and his siblings. Rachel knew this was at the root of his reluctance to consider her going into business full time. However, as Leah said you had to have faith and let God do the rest. That's what Larry needed, some faith.

"You need to consider this an opportunity, Rachel. Don't wreck it. Knock it out of the park. I know you'll do great in Anguilla," Larry stated.

She held his hands, nodded in the affirmative like she always did. She was too tired and the conversation had resurrected her headache. Choosing peace over war, she changed the subject to the football game. Sure enough, his mood became more cheery.

As he spoke animatedly about the match the previous night, Rachel allowed her thoughts to linger on the possibilities that Glow Up could bring. She just needed to have a little faith.

CHAPTER 3

MAYBE IT'S POSSIBLE

The day before the fair, Rachel enlisted Annie's help to label and package the items for her booth. While Annie reluctantly offered her help, Rachel knew she could count on her to show up.

"On a serious note, don't you have enough commitments in your life? Why are we sitting here on a Friday night eating cold pizza and labeling these bottles?" Annie complained.

Rachel shook her head and continued to focus on the task ahead. Fortunately, Larry was out with his friends, otherwise he too would have joined in on the complaint wagon.

"I didn't hear you complain when I gave you the Dior fragrance for your birthday. I think you owe a thank-you to Glow Up," Rachel replied. She knew that would get her friend to stay silent for just a few minutes. While the silence continued, she added, "What time should I expect you tomorrow at the booth?"

Annie quickly replied, "Remember, my time isn't free. I'll be there from whatever time you need me."

Rachel chuckled because she knew Annie would be there to support her.

The following day, the two arrived early to set up the Glow Up booth. Rachel glanced around and realized she was the only vendor with a skincare line. She didn't know if she should feel excited or nervous.

When they were almost through setting up, Leah came up with a huge grin on her face. She squealed in excitement as she smelled the sample fragrances. "There's someone I'd like you to meet later. I cannot wait," she almost shouted. "How are you Annie? You still haven't accepted my invitation to come to church."

Annie smiled blandly, but didn't respond.

"How are you Rachel? It feels like we haven't spoken in days," Leah continued. They'd spoken just a day ago, but Rachel knew that she was like a sister to Leah and their conversations were always uplifting.

"I'm going to need one of each item and multiply each of those by five. Mother's Day is coming soon and just like that I've completed my shopping," Leah stated. And just like that, she scurried away to greet the other vendors at their booths.

Rachel chuckled; Leah was truly a bundle of joy and made sure that everyone was comfortable and felt her support.

"We've got thirty minutes to finish the setup, Annie," Rachel said. She smiled as Annie rolled her eyes and help stacked some lotions on the display table.

Approximately three hours into their five-hour time at the fair, Rachel saw a lady and her daughter hesitantly approaching her table. She smiled encouragingly to offer reassurance and hopefully an invitation to come. The daughter looked about six years old. Upon further scrutiny, Rachel noticed that the girl had bumps on her skin from eczema. Rachel could recognize eczema from a mile away. Her niece and nephew had the same issue. Before the mother could ask, Rachel knew what she'd offer them.

The little girl smiled shyly as her mother said, "Hi, Leah recommended that I bring Susie to your booth. As you can see, she suffers from eczema and it sometime stops her sleeping. What product would you recommend for her?"

Rachel smiled, stooped down to Susie's level, and offered one of the lollipops she had as treats for customers.

"Thank you." Susie chose a red one and her smile broadened to a grin in gratitude for her treat.

Turning to Susie's mom, Rachel said, "I know just the soap and lotion that you can use for little Susie. My niece and nephew use them all the time and now have their eczema under control."

She packaged the two items and continued, "If they don't work in three days, kindly call me. I've placed my card in the bag, and I'll refund you. When they work, give me a call also, to let me know they did." She gave Susie's mom her change, and as they walked away Susie did a little skip and hop as her mom removed the wrapper of the lollipop for her.

"You're that confident that her eczema will be treated?" Annie asked.

"Definitely. I— ," She watched Leah and a lady dressed in the most beautiful sundress she'd ever seen. As they got closer, Rachel couldn't believe her eyes. Was that who she thought it was? Sure enough, Marie Parker was making her way to the Glow Up table with Leah. Everyone knew Marie Parker. Marie was head of the leading department store in their city. Only the most highly esteemed products made it into that store.

Before she could get her thoughts together, she heard Leah say, "Marie, this is Rachel, who I've been raving to you about. You have got to try her products. Rachel this is Marie, my special guest that I had to have you meet."

Marie was staring directly at her with the most genuine smile. She gulped, found her words, extended her hand and said, "It's a pleasure to meet you. I don't know what Leah's been saying about me."

Marie chuckled and replied, "Only the best things. Apparently, if I don't try your products, I'll be in big trouble with her and not know what I've missed out on."

To answer her unanswered question, Leah said, "Marie is my old classmate, and I've had her back ever since school. So she owes me a lot." They chuckled as if on cue; they evidently had a long history together.

"So tell me about what you have here," said Marie.

Thirty minutes later, Marie not only walked away with one of each product. She'd also placed an order for fifty of each item for a special display at the department store the following week. Rachel couldn't believe what was happening.

By the end of the fair, all her product was sold. She was grateful and amazed. How could Annie and Larry not see the potential in her "hobby"? Maybe this *was* possible. Maybe she could do Glow Up full time and leave the stressful firm.

"You know, I don't say this often, but good to see that you got all your product sold today. I'm proud of you." Annie said.

Rachel couldn't believe her ears. Surely this must be a divine sign. Annie never said she was proud of anyone!

When Rachel got home, she was happy to shower and relax from her long day. She wanted to share all the excitement with Larry, but he wasn't home from the gym. She admired his dedication to working out. According to him, it helped him to detox and minimize his stress. She, on the other hand, didn't have the tenacity to keep up with the gym dedication.

Just as she was going to warm up dinner, Larry came through the door. If he'd detoxed successfully, his expression didn't show it.

"Hi hon, just in time for dinner," she said. She wasn't in the mood for tension. She was still riding the high from meeting Marie Parker.

He ignored her greeting. "When were you going to tell me that our credit card is maxed out from purchases for your supplies? Rachel, this habit is costing us and affecting our credit score." She took a deep breath so she wouldn't respond harshly to him. But before she could get a word in, Larry continued. "When are you going to start acting like we have a future ahead of us and goals that we're working on?"

Well, they were more his goals than hers, but she didn't say that out aloud. Larry was driven and focused on buying a new house. He tried to make it seem like it would be for her business as well, but she knew it was more about the status for him. His brother had also just bought a new house. On his salary alone, Larry wouldn't be able to afford the mortgage, so he kept trying to convince her it was the path they ought to take.

It was true; funding her hobby, hope-to-be-a-business had affected her credit score. When she started, she hadn't priced her products correctly. Also, she'd lost forty thousand dollars trying to secure a supplier in Cambodia in hopes of making her input costs cheaper. When that happened, she was sure that would end the relationship. She had secretly used their credit card to maintain her supplies. Evidently, she hadn't done a good enough job of hiding the credit card statements from him.

"My products sold out today, and I met Marie Parker and she wants to showcase my products at her store next week," she said, ignoring his rant and hopefully getting him to see there was potential for her products.

"You just don't care, do you?" Larry retorted.

She could tell there was nothing left to say tonight to convince him about the possibility for her business. Who could blame him? It wasn't as if she'd proved to him that it was possible. A wave of guilt washed over her.

Larry didn't join her for dinner. He mumbled something about not being hungry and spent the rest of the evening in the bedroom.

"Heya, how are you doing? The kids said to say hello to their favorite aunty," said Rebecca's voice on the phone. Talking to her was always a joy. She and Rebecca loved each other, and they didn't have the usual sibling rivalry you heard about from others. They were truly each other's best friend. However, Rachel had to admit she hadn't been very upfront with Rebecca recently because she didn't want to add any additional burden to her being a full-time mom and an amazing wife to Marcus.

"I'm alright sissy. How are you, the kids, and Marcus?" She tried to sound cheerful. Larry had basically ruined her mood and excitement to share about her encounters earlier that day.

As usual, Rebecca could tell when she wasn't feeling herself. "We're great. The kids are doing great in school, and Marcus sold five houses this week." Marcus was into real estate. He was very successful, and his income afforded Rebecca the luxury of being a full-time mom to help raise the kids and care for their home. Clearly, Rebecca loved it.

"So let's cut to the chase, what's really happening with my sister? You don't have to pretend with me sis," Rebecca said

"It's Larry again. He doesn't want me to do Glow Up, and I don't know what else to do." Rachel went on to tell her about the success she'd experienced that day, and the opportunity to get her products before others at the department store. By the time she was finished sharing, she felt better and more understood.

As only Rebecca could, she got Marcus to send Rachel some money to clear up the credit card and enough extra money to get the supplies she needed to prepare for her presentation for Marie Parker. Rachel was grateful and promised to repay it as soon as possible. Rebecca assured her there was no rush, just to promise that she'd do a great job with her presentation. Although Rachel was the older sibling and had helped to raise Rebecca, she felt like Rebecca was the one who was always taking care of her.

The following day, she paid off the credit card; she definitely wasn't going to tell Larry how she got it done. He didn't deserve an explanation after the way he'd exploded last night.

Laura was waiting for her in the office when she got back an hour later. "Where have you been? You know how much I'm counting on you for this trip to Anguilla."

Rachel had forgotten about her upcoming trip. She groaned as she realized she had to present her products to Marie on Saturday and then fly to Anguilla on Monday. It was a tight window, but she made a mental note to press forward to get it all done. When her thoughts went to Larry, she was immediately happy that she was going away from him for a few days.

Her curiosity was piqued when Laura mentioned the beautiful spa that was at the resort she was going to, and that it was one of the hallmark features of the space. Laura continued that the client was contemplating making the spa a signature at his other properties around the world. While Laura had an idea of Rachel's "hobby," Rachel knew that Laura hadn't given her this assignment to connect the two. Rachel couldn't help but feel that this was the Lord at work. Yes, she needed to work on her relationship with Him more, but this couldn't be a coincidence. She felt a twinge of excitement. Of course she'd be able to help their client; not just from the accounting side of things but from a practical standpoint of what would work as a great retreat at the spa.

After her meeting with Laura, she called Leah to thank her for introducing her to Marie Parker and also to get her weigh-in on what she'd be doing on her trip to Anguilla. Immediately, Leah told her she needed to take some of her products with her. Leah too believed that this wasn't coincidental. She told Leah about her struggles with Larry and his resistance to her doing business. As usual, Leah encouraged her to have faith. Leah passionately told her that if it was God's will for her to go into business full time; He would provide the opportunities to do so. At the end of their conversation, Rachel said a prayer. Boy, did she need this confirmation.

Later that afternoon, Rachel saw a strange number pop up on her mobile phone. She answered; it was Susie's mom calling.

"Hi, how are you? How's Susie?" Rachel asked eagerly.

"I just had to call to let you know that your products worked wonderfully on her. She's finally sleeping through the night," Susie's mom told her. She promised to get more of Rachel's products and to share her review with other moms at Susie's school.

Rachel ended the call feeling hopeful.

Her phone rang again; this time it was Larry. She was tempted to ignore him, but then, she had just prayed. She didn't want to upset God.

"Hello?"

"Hi love, I was calling to see if you were free to have dinner with me." Larry's tone was totally different from last night. He must have seen that the credit card was paid off.

"Sure, why not?" she replied reluctantly. After getting the details about where 'they'd meet, Rachel packed up and headed out.

Dinner was cordial, and she decided not to share any update about her day and the possible opportunity on her trip. If nothing else, Rachel was good at trying to keep the peace in the relationship.

To her surprise, Larry apologized for his behavior the night before. "I'm sorry, Rachel. I overreacted last night, and I know I hurt your feelings. Forgive me."

She told him she forgave him, and they went on to have a pleasant evening. By the time they got home, Rachel was so tired she just showered and went to bed. She felt a rush of mixed emotions about Larry, this upcoming trip, and the new venture with Marie Parker; somehow, she felt inside that maybe this business was possible.

CHAPTER 4

BUSINESS TRIP

Monday morning, as Rachel boarded the flight, she was so tired and made up her mind that she was going to sleep this entire five-hour flight to Anguilla, and maybe the boat ride to the resort too. Larry had dropped her off, and if she was honest with herself, she welcomed the time away from him to clear her mind and hopefully figure out what she was going to do with herself. They'd been together a long time, and she was starting to feel that she couldn't continue to sacrifice her dreams for the sake of the relationship anymore. She needed to grow.

She got settled in her seat in first class; Laura always ensured that staff was well taken care of when traveling for work duties. Rachel could tell that the flight wasn't going to be too full, and she welcomed that. Hopefully, no one would be sitting next to her, so she could get even more space to just relax and be even more comfortable on the flight.

She checked her phone for any last-minute messages before the flight. Her face lit up when she saw that Leah had sent her a psalm to encourage her about having a great trip. Annie also messaged her to say how jealous she was. Rachel couldn't help but smile; Annie was so silly. Then she saw a message from her mom, and she groaned with guilt. She hadn't really chatted with her mom for over a week. She made a mental note to call when she'd settled in at the resort. Her mom was happy about the trip and was just checking in on her.

The flight attendant came around and made sure that everyone was settled in. They made an announcement that take-off would be in fifteen minutes. This was enough time for Rachel to take out her sleep mask, her essential-oil blend that she made specifically for air travel to promote relaxation, and her travel blanket. She was just about to pull on her mask when another passenger sat in the aisle seat of her row. Only one chair separated them, and she remembered feeling happy that she'd get some space to relax even more.

Rachel jolted out of her sleep, thinking they'd landed and she'd been abandoned on the plane. She looked at her watch and realized that they were only halfway into the flight. Looking out the window, she saw the sky was clear and that they were in for a smooth ride. She chuckled at herself for jumping from her sleep. She was still tired, but the sleep had replenished some much-needed energy.

"Excuse me, have they served lunch already?" she asked the gentleman seated in her row. He was reading *Business Week* magazine.

"No, but they served snacks, and I grabbed two bags for you." He pointed at the bags of nuts and chips on the chair between them.

"Thank you," she replied gratefully. As she opened the bag of chips, she took a minute to assess her fellow passenger. He seemed not older than forty-five, and his manner was assured. Definitely an old-school upbringing to even consider taking snacks for a stranger. He wasn't overly dressed; he had on jeans and a crisp white button-down shirt. He was probably going to do business in Anguilla as well.

Just then the flight attendants began making their way through the aisle with the lunch service. Rachel chose the stewed beef with steamed greens and mashed potatoes. She didn't like carbonated drinks, so she opted for orange juice and water. Her fellow passenger decided on chicken. Suddenly aware how hungry she was, Rachel chomped into her meal,

The food was delicious, and she complimented the flight attendant. With two more hours left in the flight, Rachel decided to catch up on some reading. Her latest research was on the nutritive value of essential oils and how they could promote healing. Before settling into her book, she dabbed some of her travel oil on her temples and the insides of her hands.

"What's that glorious smell? By the way, my name is David," said her fellow passenger.

"I'm Rachel, nice to meet you and thanks again for saving me some snacks," she responded. "This is some essential oil I use to relax any time I travel."

"Does it work?"

Rachel laughed. "Definitely, I was sound asleep."

"I didn't think about getting any for flying. Where can I purchase it?"

She smiled shyly at the unexpected question. "I made it."

"Get out of here ... what? That's amazing!" David exclaimed.

"Would you like to try some?"

"Definitely. I don't get sick when I fly, but, it never hurts to feel relaxed during a flight."

She showed David the key areas to apply the oil. She normally placed it on her temple, her arms, and the side of her neck. David followed her instructions, and she could tell he was pleased with the smell and feel of the oil on his skin.

"Are you a therapist? What do you do?" David inquired. "This is really good."

Rachel chuckled. "I love everything derived from natural sources. There's more benefit for our well-being in the long run. I got interested in it because of my sensitive skin. Also, my niece and nephew are affected by eczema. So one thing led to another and other people started asking me to make them skincare products. As a matter of fact, because the products work, I took some courses and continue to do research on the benefits the oils have on our skin. This recipe is one I developed from some of my research."

She could tell he was impressed by her story, and continued, "If you rub the oil between the thumb and index finger, that's a quick way of reducing tension and stress in the shoulders."

David immediately tried it. "Are you a masseuse as well? This is working."

Again Rachel chuckled. "No, but in my research and studies, learning key body points was important to activate the full benefit of using the essential oil."

"I know that I can benefit from this, and my colleagues could too. It would really help reduce work stress."

"You can have a bottle of it if you'd like; I always take an extra one with me," she offered.

David eagerly took it from her.

It was the first time she'd got to talk about this aspect of her business with anyone, and she felt liberated. She felt at ease discussing the uses of the oils with David, and he was soaking up all she was saying. Before they knew it, the flight was getting ready to land in Anguilla. They exchanged contact information and promised to be in touch. David told her that he was eager to share the oil with his other colleagues.

After disembarking, they parted ways as they each made their way through Arrivals. As she went through the doors to look for the taxi that was scheduled to pick her up, Rachel was enthralled with the sights, smells, and sounds that vied for her attention.

The warm breeze stroked her skin. There were trees everywhere, vibrant and green—stark contrast to the tall buildings she'd left behind. The smell of the air was so refreshing. She took a deep breath and closed her eyes for two seconds. She felt like she had arrived in Paradise.

"Excuse me, are you Rachel?" a guy dressed in khakis and a tropical shirt asked. He was holding a sign with her name on a card that also read LaLuna Resorts.

"Yes that's me." He must have recognized her from the photo she'd sent ahead to the resort.

"Welcome to Anguilla. I hope you enjoy your stay with us at LaLuna Resort," he said cheerfully.

Rachel already felt welcomed; she was charmed by his warm Caribbean accent and courteous service.

The ride to the dock was about ten minutes, and he helped her take her suitcase into the boat that would take them across to the stunning island just ahead. From her quick research, LaLuna ranked number five worldwide as one of the most luxurious and all-inclusive resorts. And here she was, about to get that luxury experience.

When they got to the front desk, Rachel couldn't help but feel blown away. This was by far one of the most beautiful places she'd ever seen. It dripped opulence. Evidently, a lot of thought had gone into its design and construction. There were marble floors and walls in the lobby, plush chairs, and an airy ceiling. The landscape was well manicured and there were a lot of trees and vibrant flowers all around. The smell of the place was also inviting; she could tell that management paid attention to the details to create an amazing experience. She was given a welcome cookie and drink and checked in. Her bags were taken from her, and she was escorted to her suite. The number was 208. She loved the number eight, as it meant biblically new beginnings and the start of something new. She couldn't help but make a mental note that it could be symbolic of this journey.

When she entered the suite, Rachel was speechless. The ocean beckoned right beyond her balcony. When her butler, yes, *her* butler, had made sure she was settled in, Rachel explored the suite, stunned at the amenities. She had a Jacuzzi, a standing shower with jet sprays at every angle, marble toilet and face basin, a plush king-size bed, her own kitchenette with the finest appliances, a stocked mini bar with wine and drinks, a huge television, a private deck pool, and the list went on.

She decided to freshen up and change into something a bit more business casual. She had the meeting with her client in two hours, so she wanted to make sure she was ready. Just over an hour later, not only was she ready, but she'd got to catch up with her mom and even Rebecca. She was excited to do a video call with them to show them where she was staying.

Rachel couldn't help but long to have them there with her. Growing up, it was always the three of them. Their bond was strong and they always supported each other. Sometimes, people thought her mom looked more like her sister. She missed her family. She'd moved all the way to the East Coast for her job and in hopes she'd be able to repay her mom for all the sacrifices she'd made. Rachel knew her mom didn't require repayment, but, Rachel wanted her to know how much she was loved and appreciated. Her mom had worked two jobs and never hesitated to do additional work to ensure her daughters were provided for. If anyone deserved all good things, it was her mom.

With thirty minutes to go, Rachel decided to go ahead to the conference room to meet her client. She grew excited and anticipated the meeting ahead. Not only would she be able to help the client make a decision about the acquisition, but she knew a thing or two about what could work for the spa. She was actually planning to go there the following day.

As Rachel approached the conference room, the door was slightly ajar. She heard some muffled conversation and she could tell that people were there. She smiled to herself because she liked a client who was on time. As she opened the door and scanned the faces looking back at her, her eyes held the gaze of one familiar face. It was David! Rachel paused, stunned, how ... where ... wow ... raced through her mind.

"You must be Rachel, come on in," said one of the other two guys in the room. "I'm Jerry, manager of LaLuna Resort. Thank you for traveling all the way here to help us with this business acquisition." Rachel shook his hand. "This is Pete, my assistant manager," he went on, introducing the other gentleman. "And this is David, owner of the Oriental Group," David nodded at her.

"I met Rachel on the flight here, as it happens. She's the one who made the oils I was showing you," David said to Jerry.

Wow, Rachel thought, he must seriously like the oils to share them with the other guys.

"Come on, have a seat, Rachel," David said. "We've got quite a bit of work ahead of us to discuss this acquisition. Laura highly recommended you to help me with that decision. She didn't tell me you were also gifted in the crafting of skincare items."

Rachel smiled. "I'm excited to help you."

"As you know, I'm interested in rebranding LaLuna Resort; however, they're renowned for their spa treatments because of their use of organic essential oils. This is a feature I want to introduce to my brand worldwide," David told her.

After three hours of discussion, Rachel had helped David develop a clearer path to his vision for the acquisition. They were able to note areas that needed developing to improve the financial performance of LaLuna. It would be a great business venture. Rachel was impressed that David planned to keep all the staff at LaLuna Resort, and although the brand would change, he wanted to stay true to the culture that already existed there. As the meeting progressed, Rachel couldn't help but wonder how he was able to be so relaxed and comfortable as a businessman.

"Laura never lets me down. I'm really happy she chose you to work on this project," David said. "Rachel, I want you to know that we're also very interested in your products to add to our line of skincare here at the resort."

Rachel couldn't believe her ears. Had she heard correctly? "Excuse me? What did you say?"

"When I got here, I showed Jerry the relaxation oil; we shared it with the staff at the spa, and everyone agrees there's something amazing about this product. We want to explore what else you have on offer so we can determine how to proceed. Do you produce them in bulk?" David replied.

She looked at the other two guys in the room; they were nodding agreement and smiling.

"Yes, David told us about the technique you used with the palms of the hand for relaxation. That's an acupressure method. We also practice that type of therapy here. How soon can we have some more of your products to try?" Jerry asked.

This must be divine intervention, Rachel thought. She had samples of her different products with her in her suite. She shared that with the guys, and they decided they would transform the living area of her suite into a mini-therapy session for a few staff and selected guests to try her products. Rachel couldn't believe this was happening. Now, she was so glad Leah had encouraged her to bring her products along. She couldn't help but think about her room number, 208. The number eight was really symbolic biblically meaning born again in reference to Jesus' resurrection. For her, eight was really symbolic of what was about to take place for her in Anguilla; the birthing of Glow Up.

They arranged to start the session at 6:00 p.m. just before dinner. Rachel laid out her products. When the time arrived, with the assistance of two other spa staff, she had the attendees try out her relaxation oils, body lotions, and skin scrubs. She also gave them soap samples. The reviews were nothing less than exceptional. Everyone loved the products. In what seemed like just moments, the session concluded and everyone departed for dinner.

"I'd like you to join me for dinner if you don't have any other plans," David said.

She happily agreed and promised to meet him in an hour's time after she'd refreshed herself.

Rachel didn't return to her suite until 11:00 p.m. Dinner was delicious, and she and David talked for a long time about business. She gleaned so much from him, and she admired his tenacity in the business world. He'd started his business at the age of twenty, and his dreams were huge but not daunting to him. He had faith and believed that he was able to achieve them, and bit by bit he did. The fact that he believed in God further impressed her. She didn't think someone like him would be a Christian. The more she talked to David, the more she liked him.

When she got back to her room, Rachel sat on her bed and cried. This trip couldn't be coincidental. Her passion for her skincare line just kept growing, and hearing the amazing reviews gave her courage that her product was worth more than she'd ever believed. If she'd learned anything from David tonight, it was to believe in herself and that she was deserving of great accomplishments. She'd never looked at it like that before. She was always worried about what other people would think, and if she had what it took to launch out on her own and be successful.

One of the things that David said that struck her was that she shouldn't hide her gifts or suppress them. He reminded her that the Bible said her gifts would make room for her and bring her before great men. She couldn't believe the seeming irony of that. Here she was in a luxurious resort, and this billionaire wanted to purchase her skincare line.

Right there and then Rachel determined that she was going to launch her business. She was going to take a chance on her own self. She'd helped other people for years in their businesses through accounting and other practical advice, and it was her time now. Her mind turned to Larry and his resistance. According to David, in business, you have to align yourself with people who share your vision. As difficult as it might be, she decided, she wasn't going to fight with Larry anymore. Either he supported her or he didn't. It was time for Rachel to start being present and there for Rachel.

She settled into bed and, like never before, poured her heart out to God about every concern, dream, and goal that was on her mind. She felt a sense of peace as she drifted off to sleep. The number eight filled her dreams.

CHAPTER 5

CHARGED AND READY

The five days in Anguilla flew by. Rachel got an opportunity to visit the spa. LaLuna Resorts spared no expense in making sure their guests felt relaxed and comfortable. She spent time with the staff and got a deeper understanding of what they looked for in their skincare products.

David also spent time with her to create a work plan on how she'd mass produce her line. As a matter of fact, he was going to invest in her start up. He believed in her product that much. She had a lot of work ahead of her when she returned home, but she was charged and ready.

The plan was to find a studio space big enough to set up her production and accommodate a few staff. In three months, she'd launch Glow Up and resign from her job. That would give her enough time to transition into doing her business full time. Of course, David didn't know about Larry, but she'd deal with Larry on her own.

Rachel and David were companions again on the return flight. They spent the time discussing business and plans for the months ahead. The conversations with David were so easygoing that Rachel couldn't stop thinking about how blessed she was to have met him. When they landed, they exchanged pleasantries and set a date to get in touch.

She took a taxi home because Larry was in a meeting at his office. She didn't mind because she wanted to savor her solitude for just a bit longer. When she got to the apartment, she took a minute to soak in the trip and prepare mentally for all she had ahead. She was excited to share all that had transpired with her mom, her sister, and Leah. That same excitement wasn't there when she thought about Larry.

As she took a look around the apartment, Rachel reminisced about when she and Larry had just moved in together. They'd been filled with excitement about their future; he wanted to be in top management at his marketing firm and he envisioned that she'd become a partner at her accounting firm. Even then, although he verbally supported her making her skincare products, he never saw it as being a viable business. For years, she'd kept her dreams to herself because she valued his opinion and didn't feel confident that she had what it took to be successful. However, over the years, with great reviews and people like Leah and her sister recommending her, Rachel began to get a different perspective of what she could do.

If she was honest with herself, she knew that her relationship with Larry no longer brought her joy. How could he say he loved her but be so negative toward something that she was evidently passionate about. She knew that deep down he didn't esteem her craft because it wasn't something he could boast about to his family. Being in a career where he was highly esteemed was important to him, a major accomplishment compared to what his siblings had achieved.

Rachel had spoken to Leah about Larry, and she knew that it was time to move on. She'd held on as long as she could, but this was her time to pursue the vision in her heart. She was thinking about how to break the news to him when she heard the keys in the front door.

"Hey you," Larry said as he walked in.

"Hey," she responded. She could already tell that something was on his mind based on his body language. Larry began pacing back and forth.

This must be serious. she thought.

"Rachel, we cannot continue to be together if you're going to defy me," Larry said agitatedly. "You didn't expect me to find out that you borrowed money from your sister to purchase more products? When are you going to understand that this business you so badly want to pursue isn't going to work?"

"I ..." Rachel began, but Larry cut her off.

"You'd be better off at the accounting firm. We have goals, and I'm not going to let you mess that up for me," Larry stated fiercely. This was the most upset she'd ever seen him.

"We have goals or do you mean *you* have goals? When has anything around here ever been about me? It's always been about what Larry wanted to achieve," Rachel retorted. "Do you even care about how I feel and *my* dreams? You're the only one who doesn't believe in me."

"I'm the only one who's honest with you."

"I can't believe you're saying this to me after hearing all the positive reviews I've received. You know what? Maybe it's time we parted ways. Evidently this situation is making a rift in our relationship." She could tell he didn't expect her response, but she held herself together. It was time for her to start standing up for what she believed in and start putting herself first.

There was an awkward pause, and for a minute it seemed like time froze. Rachel could tell that he was evaluating her response and wondering what to do. He stood there with a puzzled look on his face because in all the years of their relationship, she rarely spoke up. She didn't move, reluctant to say anything first. After about five minutes, Larry shrugged his shoulders and stormed off to their room.

Emotions brimmed to the surface as tears welled up in her eyes. She would *not* let him see her cry. She picked up her car keys and decided that she was going to visit Leah. She needed someone to talk to, and Leah was perfect.

Forty minutes later, Rachel was on Leah's couch and pouring out everything that had happened on the trip and her blowout with Larry. Leah listened intently and in silence to all she said, and Rachel, from experience, knew she was taking time to process.

Finally, Leah spoke. "Rachel, you've got to pursue your dream. That much I know. You cannot toss this opportunity out the door," Her voice was calm and assured. "I'm sorry this is happening with Larry, but somehow you have to reiterate to him how much this means to you. Maybe if you tell him about the opportunity that you now have, and David, he'll have a change of heart."

"I don't know, Leah. He doesn't support me when it's a smaller gig, why should I trust him now that I have this bigger opportunity?"

"Well, sometimes people don't believe in your vision until they see it working. Tell him; he may have a change of heart," Leah gently insisted.

Her friend had a point. Rachel hadn't given Larry a chance to believe that the business was feasible. She'd borrowed money from her family and was currently behind on some of her bills. Maybe, if she could prove to him that the business was credible, he would feel confident in her, and they might have a chance after all.

Rachel spent another sixty minutes at Leah's house before she reluctantly went home. She wasn't convinced that the conversation with Larry would work, but she was willing to try. She picked up some Chinese food, hoping it would show she was willing to work things out.

When Rachel got home, Larry was sitting at the island looking deflated. He gazed at her silently as she placed their dinner on the countertop.

"I met an investor who's going to invest and help me promote my business. He already committed to selling the products at all his spa locations in the US, UK, and Caribbean," Rachel blurted out before Larry could say a word.

He looked stunned. She went on to share her trip with him and all that David had promised. Rachel could tell that he didn't expect any of what she was saying. He sat there speechless and occasionally fidgeting with a fork on the table. After she finished speaking, Larry came around to where she was standing and pulled her in for a hug. Now Rachel was stunned, she didn't expect a hug and although she hugged him back, it was hesitantly.

"If this is what you really want to do, I'm not going to be in your way. Hopefully with this investment, things can turn in a positive direction."

That was unexpected, but she was happy that he seemed to be on board finally. She returned his hug again and began setting the table for dinner.

The following morning, the sound of the alarm jolted her awake. Thankfully, she remembered it was Saturday before scampering into the shower to prepare for work. She lay back against her pillows and reflected on everything that had transpired. Room 208 at the LaLuna resort would stay etched forever in her mind. She knew in her belly that business was not going to be the same. It wasn't David, it wasn't the investment, nor the opportunity to be featured at the spa; it was simply that what transpired in Room 208 had had a huge impact on how she saw herself. People actually loved her products and felt great after using them. After years of hiding, of being unable to see the value in either her products or herself, a new and different Rachel was emerging like a butterfly from a cocoon, She felt charged and ready to give herself a chance. She was the one that everyone came to for advice and encouragement in their ventures. Now it was time that she showed up for herself. Somehow, this morning, everything felt like it was where it should be at last: Larry was now supportive, she had David's backing, Leah was praying for her, she felt confident, and she knew exactly what she was working toward.

Last night during dinner, Larry had mentioned a listing with several advertisements for vacant spaces that might be suitable for her setup. She planned to visit at least three during the day. Not only did she have to visit them, but she looked forward to bring her sister and mom up-to-date with all that transpired. Rachel could count on them at any time to support her, and she was very grateful for them.

Monday morning, Laura was waiting for Rachel in her office. She looked very pleased and welcomed her with a big smile. She must have spoken to David, Rachel thought.

"Congratulations Rachel, I've heard nothing but rave reviews from David," she said confirming Rachel's thoughts. "He was impressed and will continue to do business with us. He also mentioned that he would be acquiring LaLuna Resort."

Rachel smiled. David had asked her not to discuss their new business venture with Laura.

"Yes, the resort has the potential for growth and will align well with the other properties he already owns," Rachel responded.

"I'm so happy for him. He's such a hard worker and so ambitious. I'm glad this is working for him," Laura said as she placed some new files on Rachel's desk. "I have some other work I'd like you to start with as soon as you complete your report."

As Laura was turning to leave, she said, "I guess I'll have to work on promoting you soon."

Rachel didn't know how to respond, so she didn't. It had been a few years since Laura had promised a promotion.

"Laura, before you go, there is something I must tell you."

Laura paused and turned back. "What's up?"

"I'm grateful for all this company has done for me, but I think it's time for me to do something different. I'm going to take a chance on myself," Rachel told her.

There was a momentary pause before Laura said, "Rachel, you're a good woman, and you've been so loyal to the firm and our customers. I appreciate all you've done. If this is what you need to do, I'm here for you. Give it a try. If you change your mind, you can always come back."

Rachel couldn't believe her ears; this was the first time she'd ever heard Laura express how she felt about her. Amazing, she thought.

"When do you leave?" Laura asked.

"I have to write it officially, but it will be in three months."

"You have my support. Just let me know what you need," Laura told her and continued out of the room.

Rachel sat at her desk for a few minutes trying to make sense of what had just happened. She hadn't known what to expect from Laura, but she was happy to know that her boss was supportive of her new venture.

Wow, just wow, Rachel thought to herself.

Her phone vibrated. She glanced at the screen —David. She was so stunned by how everything had come together that she'd forgotten their appointment.

She paused and then answered. "Hi, David, how are you?"

"Hi, Rachel, I'm great. It's great to hear your voice as well. How have you been?"

"Unbelievable. I'm so excited to get started on our project. I say our because I wouldn't be this far if it wasn't for your support," she gushed.

"You're being too kind. You're where the talent lies, Rachel. I'm just here to see that you don't give up on yourself," he said.

Rachel was grinning from ear to ear. David was unlike any other man she'd ever met. He was undeniably humble, calm, and very easy to talk to. She was still amazed that she'd met him and this was all happening. She had to admit she did find him a little attractive too, but she was determined to focus on the goal ahead. Besides, she was with Larry.

"I have some good news," she said. She brought David up to date with the spaces she'd found, the suppliers, the costs involved in getting the basic material arranged, and even about Laura's support. She didn't mention Larry. She'd never told David about him. Not that it mattered. Their phone call lasted almost an hour, but at the end of it she felt ready, charged, and in the right place at the right time.

When she checked the time, she realized how quickly it had passed. With all that was happening, she decided it was a good day to have lunch alone. As she looked outside, the weather agreed with her thoughts. She grabbed her bag and headed to the park with an extra pep in her step.

CHAPTER 6

AN UNEXPECTED EVENT

Rachel stood looking at her office space in flames. This couldn't be happening. She'd only rented it two months ago, and a load of delayed supplies had just shown up after a month-long delay. She'd been working feverishly that afternoon when an electrical fire broke out. She did what she could to salvage some materials, but only so much was possible.

She watched, weeping, as the firemen tried to out the fire. So upset was she that she didn't realize Leah was standing next to her until her friend pulled her in for a hug. She all but lost it then as she poured out even more tears. How could this be happening?

Larry had ended their relationship three weeks ago, claiming that she wasn't spending enough time with him and that the business was more consuming than he'd imagined. She had to find another apartment, her suppliers were late, and she was worried that she wouldn't meet the deadlines needed to stock the LaLuna Resort. David was planning a grand relaunch of his brand, and he wanted her products installed by then. Although Laura stated that she supported her, Rachel was falling behind on her work because she was trying to juggle both the deadlines at the firm and her personal deadline for the products.

As if that wasn't enough, her mom had fallen ill and Rachel and Rebecca had shared taking care of her for about two weeks. She loved her mom and would do anything for her. As a matter of fact, she was Rachel's inspiration for doing this business. Rachel dreamed of being able to take her mom on vacations and treat her well as a show of gratitude for all the sacrifices she'd made for her and Rebecca.

Rachel was used to pressure, but this fire was all it took to unravel all the emotions she'd been suppressing as she worked toward her goals. She was determined to succeed and to take a chance on herself. How could she come back from this? What was going to happen to all the money that David had invested so far?

It wasn't until 2:00 a.m. that the firemen completely extinguished the fire. After the officers questioned her and filed their reports, she was walking back to where Leah stood when she fainted.

***

Beep, beep, and beep were the first sounds Rachel heard when she woke up in the hospital.

"Hey you," Leah calmly said next to her.

She turned her head to see her friend sitting in the chair next to the bed.

"I hope you got some much-needed sleep. You've been out for eight hours." Leah smiled and then said, "You'll be alright, Rachel. God brought you through. You will be alright."

Rachel's heart sank, and she felt tears well up as she remembered the fire. "My mom and sister. I have to call them."

"Don't worry, I called them and let them know what happened and that you'll be alright." Rebecca's flying in later today, and David said he'll come tomorrow. He has to cancel his flights to LaLuna, but he's coming."

Rachel didn't ask how Leah was able to convey all that information, but she knew that she was grateful for her friend.

Leah stayed with her until Rebecca arrived later that day. The doctors told her that she needed more rest and explained that she fainted because of dehydration. They advised her to take a week off to build her energy and recuperate.

When she and Rebecca got to her apartment, she was happy she wasn't alone. Rebecca immediately got to making them dinner and made sure that Rachel didn't lift a finger to do any work. Again, Rachel felt nothing but gratitude.

"Want to catch a rerun of *Friends*? When was the last time you looked at the television?" Rebecca asked.

Rachel laughed. Rebecca knew the answer to that question. Rachel didn't watch the television often. Rebecca fixed Rachel a plate of homemade lasagna and a tall glass of freshly squeezed lemonade. Rachel didn't realize how hungry she was until she started eating. She got a second helping, and they spent a few hours just laughing at their favorite teen-years show.

"Thank you, sis," Rachel said as they got ready to retire for the evening.

"Don't mention it. This is what we are, sis—family." Rebecca hugged her. "I'm just happy you're alright. I love you. Get some rest; you have me to pamper you all week long. You just let me know if you need anything."

"Anything?" Rachel teased. They both laughed as they went to their separate rooms.

The next day, Rachel was ready to talk and she did. She told Rebecca everything that had happened. Sure enough, her sister was supportive and had nothing but good words of advice and reassurance to give her.

Leah came by and, of course, she and Rebecca hit it off. You'd think they'd known each other for a century. Rachel started to feel a bit better with them around and fussing over her to make sure she was alright.

Inside, she dreaded talking to David. She hadn't talked to him yet, and honestly, she could wait. She didn't know what to tell him, and she couldn't bear if he was disappointed with her. He truly had motivated her to come this far. While she knew she couldn't be blamed for the fire, she still felt responsible.

She was relieved when he didn't show up later that day and didn't contact her for the next three days.

On the fifth day after the fire, the door bell rang, but before she could get to it, she heard Rebecca greeting someone. When she got there, standing talking animatedly with her sister was David.

As soon as he saw her, he came up to her and gave her a huge hug. "How are you doing?" There wasn't an ounce of disappointment in his voice or expression. "I wish I could have been here sooner, but I wanted to get some things done and clear my schedule for the next five days so I could be here with you."

Rachel was stunned. David, as usual, was doing more than she was accustomed to. Before she could respond, Rebecca invited him in for lunch. Leah was also coming in a couple of hours. Well, at least they'd all get to meet the man who'd taken a chance on her and given her the courage to go after her dreams.

David spent the next five days helping after Rebecca left. Every day, he showed up to her door at 9:00 a.m. He insisted that she had to pick up from where she left off, and his support helped her stay focused. From their conversations so far, there wasn't any disappointment, just acceptance that the fire took place and determination to reach the goal they'd set months ago.

"David, I still don't get it. Why me? What do you see in me? How can you remain so optimistic?" Rachel asked him on the last evening before he returned home.

"It's because I see a lot of myself in you," he responded.

She was totally shocked. "What do you mean?"

David told her that growing up he lived with his uncle who was a shrewd businessman. He believed that everyone had what it took to be a successful business owner. Even when David was very young, his uncle practically forced him to think of ways to make money. David was very shy. He lived with his uncle because his dad was very abusive to him and his mother, so his mother sent David to live with her brother. Due to the years of abuse, David wasn't very confident. He always shied away from communicating with anyone.

However, his uncle helped him through his fears. He told David that everyone had some sort of fear and the only way to overcome it was to confront it. His uncle told him to pretend that whatever fear he had was a person and to write down everything that fear told him. After writing it down, he told him to write down the positive side of what fear had told him. So if fear told him he wasn't strong enough, write down that he was strong enough and repeat it to himself every time he felt fear creeping up on him.

After implementing that, David was able to be a star athlete in high school, and he followed after his uncle's entrepreneurial spirit. David also had the personal goal of helping anyone that he saw needed that extra courage to go after their dreams.

He further elaborated that when he met her on their flight, he was truly impressed with her product but regretted not getting her contact information. As a result, when they met up at LaLuna Resort and he realized she was the one there to assist him with his acquisition, he wasn't going to let the opportunity go to help her achieve her goal.

Listening to David's story, Rachel couldn't help but feel further impressed by him. She felt nothing short of gratitude.

"I am truly grateful David; you really can't imagine how much this means to me," she said

"That's why you cannot allow this seeming setback to make you give up on your dreams. Brush yourself off and keep going," David encouraged.

On Sunday morning, when Rachel got up, the apartment was super quiet compared to the past two weeks with Rebecca, Leah, and David being in and out and making sure that she was okay and on her feet again. Rachel finally had the strength she needed to go forward. Thankfully, everything wasn't destroyed by the fire. From her analysis, the majority of her inventory was still stuck in shipment. The delay had turned out to be a good thing after all.

Also, she and David agreed it was time to enlist some help. With the output that was needed, it was time she recorded her recipes, developed a system, and hired staff. All of this scared Rachel, but, she knew it was time to implement the necessary steps to get her to her goal.

David called her the following morning with some great news: the insurance company was going to cover the loss of the studio and the damaged inventory. In addition, they were going to compensate for the time lost from work and give her enough finances to get a new studio.

This was the breath of fresh air she needed to start her morning. It was also her last day on the job. Laura had planned a small farewell party, and although Rachel felt a little sad to be leaving the familiar environment after a lot of years serving, she was relieved to be going onto her own venture.

CHAPTER 7

GROWTH/NEW CHAPTER

Three months later, Rachel stood in the middle of her new studio which was abuzz with eight production employees, a manager, a delivery guy, a receptionist, and of course, herself as the owner. She couldn't begin to imagine what life would have been like if she hadn't been willing to go out on a limb for her dream. Not only was she in a better space mentally and physically, she was also doing well financially. There were now no more limits to what she felt she was able to achieve.

Since opening her new studio, she was not only able to make the deadline for the items for LaLuna Resort, but she was able to secure other wholesale opportunities with other major hotels and skincare companies. Her sales were on the incline.

For the first time in her career, Rachel was able to take an official vacation to Italy for her fortieth birthday. Rebecca had encouraged her to do something for herself for once. Leah also insisted that even if it meant filling in for Rachel, it was important she do something for her birthday. So Rachel booked a five-day visit, and she had fun. She thoroughly enjoyed traveling to an unknown city and going to iconic landmarks that she'd only read about in books. Also, it was one of the countries she'd written on her list of places to visit, many years ago from her first business trip.

"Excuse me, Rachel." Her receptionist's voice jolted her from the daydream. "David is on the line."

"Put the call through to my office." She smiled as she heard David's voice on the other end of the line. He was currently in Canada checking in on two locations in his hotel chain. They'd secretly begun dating a month ago. Another thing she hadn't expected or seen coming. However, she must admit, she felt as comfortable with him as if she'd known him all her life. Their friendship was undeniable, and she felt deep down that they would be fine together.

"How are you? Is everything well?" Rachel asked him.

"Everything's well with me. I'm just checking in on my favorite lady to make sure all's well with her," David said.

She smiled; she had grown accustomed to him always making sure that she was okay. "It is. Everyone's doing what they need to, and Macy's called wanting to feature our brand in their Christmas list of must-have gifts," she told him.

"Congratulations! Now, madam CEO, we both know how hard it is to tear you away from your work. Don't forget to book the flight for the surprise trip to LaLuna next month for your mom, Rebecca, Leah, and Annie."

"Don't worry, I'll get on it after the call," Rachel promised. "Please ensure it's Room 208. I wouldn't have them stay in any other space."

"I've got you covered," David replied. "I'm flying in for a few days next week. See you then. I love you, Rachel."

"I love you too, David," she replied as she hung up the phone.

Annie was now living on the other side of the country. They remained in touch, and she was coming to LaLuna with Rachel and her family. Rachel and Annie went all the way back to high school, and she wanted to treat Annie for being a great friend over the years.

Leah was going as well. Leah was a real trooper who went beyond the call to make sure that Rachel was okay. She was happy to have connected with her, and their relationship continued to blossom.

Of course, she was taking her mother and Rebecca. Although the business was relatively new, Rachel's profit margin allowed her to repay Rebecca and clear up her debts. She was able to also aide Rebecca in taking care of their mom by hiring a full time housekeeper, something she hadn't been able to do before.

Rachel was excited about the trip. She was finally able to show in a great way how much she appreciated these women in her life as they helped her along her journey.

Rachel's products were in stores online, in major department stores, and a few major hotels. She anticipated further expansion in the hotel chains because of the incredible referrals she kept getting from her customers.

As a matter of fact, the surprise trip was part business, to launch a new line of products at LaLuna Resort, where her journey had begun. Unfortunately, David wouldn't be there, and that was why he'd encouraged her to take the ladies with her.

As Rachel reminisced on how she'd got to this point, she remembered it like it was yesterday: Room 208, LaLuna Resort, David asking her a pointed question, "If you're not willing to take a chance on yourself, who will?" She'd felt nervous about showcasing her samples to him and the other resort managers. Not only were they impressed, but they wanted her to provide them with more samples. They didn't question her past or ability; they just saw her product and wanted more.

When she'd explained her situation to David, he immediately offered her his assistance and invested in her brand. She had since also repaid him his investment, and her business was being run solely on her investments. She was grateful to have been able to accomplish all that she had thus far.

The following two weeks, the ladies had flown in to meet her in New York, and she told them about the surprise trip they were about to take the following day. As expected, they were totally surprised and excited. Rachel provided everything that they would need for travel, and then they jetted off on a chartered flight.

Every time she visited LaLuna Resort, she remain convinced that it was one of the most picturesque places she had ever been to. The food, activities, and amenities were consistent and did not disappoint. Everyone in her party was thoroughly satisfied.

The day of the launch was finally here. They didn't know until that morning that they were also there to support her in her new product launch at LaLuna Resort. Rachel had ensure that they'd spent time sailing, at the spa, snorkeling and just having a great time.

"Hey guys, I'm going ahead to make sure everything is set up. You have an hour and you can come meet me there," Rachel told her family and friends.

"We'll be there soon," Rebecca said.

As Rachel walked to the spa, she was excited because not only would the new line be launched, but they were going to give trial samples to guests at the resort.

The ceremony began promptly at 8pm. Rachel scanned the room and smiled. There were a lot of people there for this special occasion. The program had speeches from the Resort Manager, Rachel, and even reviews from guests who had tried the products at the Spa. The Master of Ceremony was announcing a feature guest speaker, Rachel looked up in time to see none other than David, heading toward the platform she sat on. She shook her head and smiled. He never ceased to surprise her.

He gave a mischievous smile to her as he took the stage to give his speech. He spoke about her brand and how important it was to LaLuna. Then came time to sample the products. All the guests had nothing but great feedback for her.

After the launch, she and the ladies headed to the private dinner reception that was being held in her honor. She didn't get to catch up with David after his speech, but he told her he would meet up with them at dinner. She was secretly looking forward to poking fun at David for surprising her.

Dinner was earmarked at the Asianne restaurant. As soon as they got there, Rachel saw a huge sign with the words "*Will you marry me?*" She immediately wondered if they had gone to the wrong dinner hall and also who was the lucky girl being proposed to ... then her eyes connected with David's and he started moving across the room toward her. That was when the other ladies chimed in from behind her, shouting SURPRISE!

What? How could they surprise her on the surprise trip that she'd planned for them? As a million thoughts and unanswered questions raced through her mind, David knelt before her.

"Rachel, I love you. You are the kindest and most sincere woman I've ever known. You are resilient and I see nothing less than the best for you. You've brought so much joy to me from the moment we first met and I want to continue on this journey by your side as your husband. Will you marry me?" he asked.

Rachel started to cry, laugh, and smile as she said YES. This was really happening; she launched her business, it was doing well and now the man who saw the best in her was asking her to be his wife. Everything was really working together for her good.

David placed the most beautiful diamond ring on her left ring finger and kissed her right there and then. She was going to be his wife.

The ladies took turns hugging her and congratulating both her and David on this step. Rachel learned later that David had told her mom and Rebecca his intentions and got their blessing. Nothing short of gratitude is what Rachel felt for all that was happening for her. Who best to be her husband than her biggest cheerleader? And that was surely who David was to her.

Rachel and David got married three months later. It was a very small, elegant and intimate wedding at no other location than LaLuna Resort.

You guessed it right...they honeymooned in Room 208.

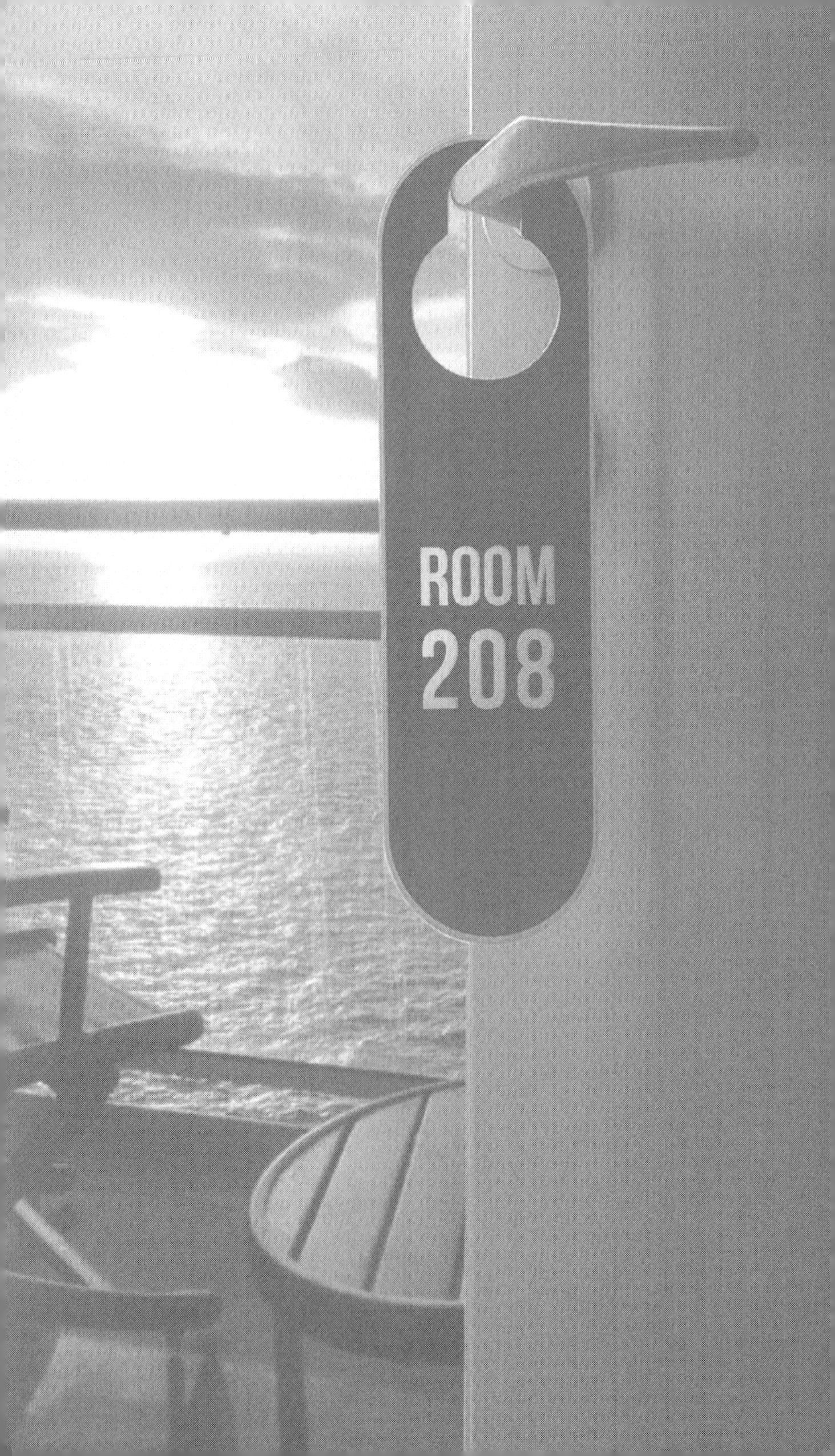
ROOM
208

Made in the USA
Columbia, SC
23 October 2022